SWAPPING HIS BRIDE
MAIL ORDER BRIDES OF FORT RIGGINS

~

SUSANNAH CALLOWAY

Tica House Publishing

Sweet Romance that Delights and Enchants!

Copyright © 2022 by Tica House Publishing LLC

All rights reserved.

No part of this book may be reproduced in any form or by any electronic or mechanical means, including information storage and retrieval systems, without written permission from the author, except for the use of brief quotations in a book review.

PERSONAL WORD FROM THE AUTHOR

Dearest Readers,

Thank you so much for choosing one of my books. I am proud to be a part of the team of writers at Tica House Publishing who work joyfully to bring you stories of hope, faith, courage, and love. Your kind words and loving readership are deeply appreciated.

I would like to personally invite you to sign up for updates and to become part of our **Exclusive Reader Club**—it's completely Free to join! We'd love to welcome you!

Much love,

Susannah Calloway

VISIT HERE to Join our Reader's Club and to Receive Tica House Updates!

https://wesrom.subscribemenow.com/

CONTENTS

Personal Word From The Author	1
Chapter 1	4
Chapter 2	12
Chapter 3	19
Chapter 4	26
Chapter 5	35
Chapter 6	43
Chapter 7	54
Chapter 8	62
Chapter 9	68
Chapter 10	74
Chapter 11	86
Continue Reading…	97
Thanks For Reading!	100
More Mail Order Bride Romances for You!	101
About the Author	103

CHAPTER 1

The soft summer sun of an early spring day lit up the landscape around Circle Moss, and the verdant green of the pastures seemed to glow in the light. Far off to the south, longhorn cattle lowed and champed, seeming small and easy to manage in the distance. The ranch was peaceful, waking up from the long winter and welcoming the foretaste of summer heat.

Adrian Moss, his arms folded, and his narrow frame leaned back against the side of the barn, smiled at the sight, but it was more from habit than anything. His hazel green eyes scarcely saw the details of the beauty in front of him. He was contemplating a different sort of beauty – the beauty of the woman he was going to marry.

The fact he had not yet seen her in person meant little. He was sure she would be beautiful, just as he was sure they would love each other dearly as soon as they laid eyes on each other. How could it be any other way?

That, at least, was what the agency would have him believe.

Mrs. Gibbons, of the Gibbons and MacNenny Matrimonial Agency over in Hamilton, had assured him of as much, many times over.

"We are in the business of making matches that are not just a matter of a husband in need of a wife, Mr. Moss," she had told him, chin lifting and nostrils flaring with the glory and honor of her chosen profession. "We are in the business of making matches that result in the union of two souls."

Mrs. Gibbons' flowery expressions notwithstanding, Adrian had to admit to himself the idea was immensely appealing. Here he was, twenty-eight years old and one of a scattered handful of men his age in the area who had not yet found a wife, settled down, and started a family. Unmarried women in and around Fort Riggins, Montana, were at a premium due to their rarity. Even widows below forty were highly prized. Any girl who had a husband who was accident-prone or a bit on the sickly side was kept note of, just in case. It made sense, overall, that the matrimonial agency would open up in Hamilton, the county seat. Word had gotten around, as it tended to do in small communities without many hobbies readily available, and before long, Adrian's foreman, Stu

Demont, was nudging Adrian in the ribs and saying, "What do you reckon, Ade? 'Bout time that we settled down?"

Adrian couldn't help but grin at the memory. His foreman was a few years older than Adrian himself, and even more settled a bachelor. Stu was a good man, though, with a good head on his shoulders. He'd served as the ranch foreman for ten years, before Adrian had even taken over after his father passed away. Stu was dedicated, knowledgeable, and a workhorse. Adrian figured it would take someone truly special to make him get down on one knee, matrimonial agency or no matrimonial agency.

Still, the suggestion had stuck with him. He'd thought of it off and on for a few weeks, and the more he pondered over it, the better he liked the idea. He'd always been something of a romantic, though it wasn't the normal thing for a man – especially a rancher, who needed to be solemn and focused – to get carried away with moonlit dreams. Mrs. Gibbons' repeated reassurances that Adrian would find the one he loved, right out of the gate, were too much for him to turn down.

And now, he knew the name of his soon-to-be-beloved: Linda Emmerson.

Miss Linda Emmerson, twenty-five, a nurse by trade, brought up in Boston, Massachusetts, and to be betrothed to a rancher in Fort Riggins, Montana. She must be an adventurous spirit, he thought fondly. The details were somewhat vague other than her name, age, and occupation, but he could picture her all too clearly in his mind. On the slim side, slight and dainty – perhaps with wide blue eyes and golden blonde hair…

She would sit across from him at the supper table and smile with promise in her eyes.

They would get married in the little church in Fort Riggins, married on a morning in early May, and she would clasp his hands and look up into his eyes and softly promise, "I do…"

"Ade. Hey, Ade. Adrian!"

The increasingly loud calls of his foreman brought him back to reality with a thump. The thump, in this case, was delivered by Stu, who clapped him on the back, startling him greatly. He hadn't realized quite how deeply into his reverie he had descended; his foreman walked right up to him without him even noticing.

Maybe he was more of a romantic than he was willing to let on, even to himself.

"You all right, boss?" Stu stepped back and eyed Adrian. "You look a little dazed."

Adrian shook his head.

"I'm fine. I was just daydreaming, I guess."

"I hope you weren't daydreaming about getting through another week without losing a longhorn," Stu said, his tone turning a bit grim. Adrian sighed and rubbed his face with both hands.

"Another one?"

Stu nodded. "Out in the south field. Same as the others."

Adrian folded his arms, squinting in the sun, turning to look south as though he could see all the way to the scene of the crime. "I don't like to do it, but we're going to have to set traps if we keep losing them to the wolves."

"I don't care about the wolves so much," Stu said, "as long as we can keep any nosy wanderers from stumbling across 'em. One wolf gets caught in it, I'll bet the rest will shy off."

"It'll be worth it, then. With the calves on in spring, we can't take the risk."

Springtime was birthing season on the ranch, and it looked to be a bumper crop this year, with six calves already wobbling around their mothers on spindly legs in the barn and another three due in the next week or so. It wasn't unusual for Circle Moss to produce twenty calves each season, which helped to keep the numbers up. But if the wolves continued their tyranny, there was no way to guarantee the safety of the young animals.

Stu nodded.

"I'll stop in at the feed store tomorrow when I go to the post office and pick up some traps."

"Heading into town again? You just picked up supplies yesterday."

"I know, but I've owed my little sister a letter for weeks now," Stu said, grinning ruefully. "She's havin' a hard time ever since Aunt Mabel passed. The old girl was our only living relative, and Clara doesn't like living alone."

"Well, why doesn't she come here, then?" Adrian had never met Stu's 'little sister,' but he had a pretty clear idea of what she'd be like. A miniature Stu, no doubt, tall and thin and with midnight-black hair and black eyes to match. It was impossible to know her age without asking Stu point-blank; there was something of an age difference between the siblings, and to hear Stu talk about her, it sounded like she was only about twelve years old. Adrian didn't think that could be right, though – it must just be a product of Stu being a protective older brother. As a protective older brother himself, Adrian could sympathize.

"Say, there's a thought," said Stu, rubbing his chin. "'Course, it would be a big change for her."

"She could stay with you in the cottage. There's that spare room we could fix up."

"And she'd be handy around the ranch, too," Stu said, mulling it over. "She'd earn her keep, right enough."

"Maybe she'd be company for Ma and Phoebe," Adrian said thoughtfully, and then half-smiled as thoughts of Linda

Emmerson floated back into his mind. "If they need any more company, that is."

Stu eyed him sharply.

"I'll write to her about it," he said. "Now, what's going on in your head, boss?"

Adrian opened his mouth, ready to tell his friend all about it, and then closed it again. He couldn't let on, not without telling his mother and sister first. They'd never let him hear the end of it if they found out he told Stu before them.

"Nothing much," he said, and grinned at the expression of sheer disbelief this earned him from his trusted foreman. "Nothing I can tell you right at the moment, anyhow. I've got to head back in for supper, Stu. Will you get Tommy and Bill to help you with the steer? And better get ten traps tomorrow, at least, if Mr. Wilkes has them in stock."

"Will do, boss."

Adrian waved at Stu and headed toward the ranch house, the echoes of his daydream about Linda Emmerson swirling around his mind even as he tried to concentrate on more immediate matters, such as the loss of his cattle as they were picked off, or the speculative look he'd received from his foreman. If he didn't hurry up and tell his family about Miss Emmerson, and then tell Stu right away, there would be all sorts of rumors being spread around town tomorrow. Not that he wasn't used to being the subject of gossip, at least occasionally – there really was very little to do around Fort Riggins other than chat.

Well, before too long, the townsfolk would have something solid to discuss amongst themselves. By the time mid-April rolled around, he would be heading into town to collect Miss Linda Emmerson – his bride to be, the woman of his dreams, the girl he was bound to fall in love with – from the little train station.

And the rest of the story, he was absolutely certain, would end with "and they lived happily ever after."

CHAPTER 2

Clarabelle Demont gave up on trying to fight it any longer. With her aunt's favorite apron in her hands, she sat down on the floor in the little kitchen, buried her face in the cloth, and cried.

It wasn't the first time she had given way to weeping in the past few months. But it was different this time – now, she wouldn't be forced to pull herself together with the empty hope that things would change for the better. Now, she knew exactly where she was going and what was going to change: she was trading Sandusky, Ohio, for a little town named Fort Riggins, Montana. She was trading living alone in the tiny house for living with her older brother in a cottage on a ranch. She was trading the entirety of her history up until now, centered on a house she'd lived in for her whole life, for…

Well. For the unknown.

The thought made her cry harder.

Oh, she knew things were going to get better. They could hardly get any worse. She'd never been so lonely in her whole life as she had been since her Aunt Mabel died. She couldn't remember her parents, and her brother had left their aunt's home when Clara was just eight years old. She wrote to him regularly, and he managed to write back when she nagged him enough. She loved him dearly, but – the truth was, she hardly knew him at all anymore.

What if she was making a mistake by leaving her little house, which her aunt had left to her, and going to Montana?

She sat up straight, dropping the apron in her lap, and shook her head, dashing the tears from her eyes.

"Listen to me, Clarabelle Demont," she said out loud. "There's no use in sitting here feeling sorry for yourself. If you're lonely, then take steps to solve the problem. Your brother loves you and wants to care for you. He can't come here to Sandusky – he needs to work, and his job is in Fort Riggins. You have no reason not to leave. You have a hundred reasons to go…"

Tears welled up again, but she fought them back this time. Instead, she got up off the floor, bringing Aunt Mabel's favorite apron with her, and folded it with neat, clipped movements. There wasn't much more room in the trunk that would travel with her to Fort Riggins, but she wouldn't leave Aunt Mabel's apron behind if she had to wear it the entire way.

Sometimes, it took Clara's breath away to realize how quickly, and how entirely, her life had changed. Why, it seemed like just yesterday that Aunt Mabel was sitting there at the table, mixing up bread dough with her knobby fingers, smiling at Clara as she asked for the latest news from around Sandusky. The illness that had taken the vital old woman to her eternal rest had been swift and sudden; on the whole, Clara supposed she should be grateful for it. Aunt Mabel never could stand to be sick, and even when she had taken ill every once in a while, she chafed at the necessity of staying in bed.

"The world doesn't stop moving just because I catch a little cold," she would say. "And if I don't get up and get after it, I'll be left behind."

The world that Aunt Mabel had known was largely made up of her niece and nephew, whom she had taken under her wing after the untimely death of Clara's parents. And then Stuart had left for his job in Fort Riggins, and Clara had become the center of Aunt Mabel's universe, unchallenged and unaccompanied. Perhaps that was why she felt the loss of her aunt so deeply, Clara thought – deep in her heart, she missed the feeling of being loved.

Now, there was nothing to do except to finish packing up her things, hand the keys to the house over to Mrs. Clyde, the neighbor down the street, and catch the train to Fort Riggins later that afternoon.

She wandered through the house, still clutching the apron, stopping in every room and thinking of the fond memories that had been made there. Yes, it was a simple and modest upbringing she'd had – but the love she'd felt every day of her life had made it a rich one.

Suppose she was never loved like that again?

She tried to put the thought out of her mind, but it was persistent. She knew what Mrs. Clyde would say if she told her of her worry.

The middle-aged woman had already made her thoughts on the whole subject very clear.

"Moving to live with your brother?" she had said when Clara first told her. She shook her head and tsk-tsked loudly. As a mother and new grandmother, Mrs. Clyde had very well developed tsk-tsking muscles. "Why should you do that, Miss Clarabelle?"

"He's the only family I have left, Mrs. Clyde."

"What's stopping you from making some more, then?" She sat back in her chair and eyed the befuddled expression that Clara gave her, and then sat forward again, satisfied that her young neighbor required further explanation. "You're twenty years old, Miss Clarabelle. Find yourself a husband here in Sandusky and settle down in your own little house."

Clara stared at her, wide-eyed. "I can't do that, Mrs. Clyde."

"Whyever not?" The older woman shook her head and Clara could feel another tsk-tsk coming on. "There's plenty of young bucks out there who would happily have you on their arm for the next county fair. Don't tell me you haven't noticed them gazing after you – a pretty girl like you in a town like this is like a child in a sweetshop."

Clara couldn't help but suspect that Mrs. Clyde had gotten her metaphors somewhat mixed, but her neighbor was continuing on regardless without pausing for any further input. "You could have the pick of the litter."

Clara swallowed past the lump in her throat and shook her head. "I don't want to be married, Mrs. Clyde," she said. "At least, not yet."

"You're plenty old enough, Miss Clarabelle."

"I know I am – and I'm sure I'll settle down when the time is right. But I'm not going to settle for any of the young men here in Sandusky – I know them all a mite too well. Besides, I don't trust any of them as well as I trust my brother. And I need my brother right now, Mrs. Clyde."

This interview had taken place only a month after Aunt Mabel had been laid to rest in the little cemetery outside the church. Mrs. Clyde had seen the tears that stood in Clarabelle's eyes, and her heart had softened.

"Oh, very well, then," she allowed, and patted Clara on the hand. "I still think that marrying a fine man here in Sandusky is the perfect answer to everything – but you'll do what you think best, I'm sure."

"I don't know yet if we will sell the house," Clara told her, wiping her eyes. "May I leave the keys with you until Stuart and I reach a decision?"

"For sure you may," said Mrs. Clyde, brightening up at the possibility that Clara might return. But as difficult as it was to face the reality of leaving the place where she had grown up, Clara had no intention of returning. It would be easier to sell the house later, after she had been gone for a while and had a chance to become attached to her new home at Fort Riggins.

For now, she worked up the courage to gather her things and approach the threshold of the little house.

She stopped there and turned to look down the long, cool hallway toward the kitchen that had been her Aunt Mabel's favorite room.

It was difficult to get the word out, but she managed.

"Goodbye," she whispered, and turned away, hurrying down the steps before she could change her mind.

She had a long journey ahead of her, and no clear idea of what awaited her at the end – but she knew that her brother would be there, waiting with open arms, and that was enough.

It would have to be enough.

She had nothing else, no one else, and she wanted nothing more than to not be alone any longer – and, she dared to hope, to be loved.

CHAPTER 3

The sun was heading for the horizon on another beautiful day as Adrian and Stu trudged back from the farthest field, Adrian to check on the calves in the barn and Stu to harness in the old gray mare and head into town. Stu was talking a mile a minute.

"I finally got the rest of the room cleared out for her, and Phoebe came in this morning to make up the bed. Sweet girl, your sister."

Adrian grinned.

"She is – you might never guess that she was related, huh? Took you this whole time to clear out the spare room – leaving things to the last minute, aren't you, what with your sister coming in today?"

"Oh, is that today?" Stu asked, feigning surprise. Adrian laughed. His foreman had been talking of nothing but the impending arrival of his sister for the last few days. As excited as the older man clearly was, his apprehension was just as obvious. Adrian didn't know much about Stu's past, other than the fact that his parents had died when he was quite young, and he and his sister had been raised by their Aunt Mabel. He couldn't help but be a little curious about Stu's connection with his sister, after all these years.

Well, he would find out the details soon enough. The sun in the sky marked time near four o'clock.

"You'd better be headed into town pretty soon. Train arrives at five."

"Sure will," Stu responded, but his attention was distracted by something that caught his eye as they shouldered through the final gate before the barn. "Say, it looks like that repair job that Tommy did the other day didn't stick too well. See the fence corner? It's only one stiff breeze away from falling apart."

It was true – the thick nails that Tommy had used to connect the angles of the fencing had not done their job very well. Instead of snugging the join, they had split the weather-weakened wood so that the lower part of the top rail hung loose, like a gap-jawed fish.

"That's going to need to be re-done," Adrian agreed. "I'll send Tommy out when I see him tomorrow."

"Why do that, boss, when he was the one who caused the problem in the first place?" Stu shook his head. "No, I can sort it out in a jiffy. I've got my tool bag with me, might as well do it now."

"Are you sure? You've got to pick up your sister."

"It won't take long. You head on over to the barn and see about those calves, Ade. I'll take care of things here."

Dubiously, Adrian nodded and left him behind to push on to his next task.

"At least put on some gloves," he called over his shoulder.

He didn't want Stu to be late collecting his sister, but after all, Stu was his foreman and was the most experienced of the employees at the ranch. If he couldn't do it, it couldn't be done.

The calves were doing fine, growing well and nursing heartily. Adrian pitched some hay down for the mothers and then climbed back down from the loft, leaning his folded arms across the top railing of the stalls and watching them with a smile. It was impossible not to love this part of being a rancher – maybe his peers would think less of him for having a soft spot for baby animals, but he didn't care.

He was just getting ready to head into the house when there came a yell of pain and shock from outside.

"Ade. Ade!"

He broke into a run. The voice was that of Stuart Demont.

His foreman was down on his knees near the place where Adrian had left him, bent over double, his face grimaced in pain. Adrian saw immediately what had happened – Stu had overestimated his strength or the weight of the top railing, and gravity had caught up with him. The broken fence rail, weighed down by the water it had soaked up from the recent rains, had fallen on Stu's hand, pinning it to the lower split rail. But the weight alone wasn't enough to cause this level of pain, nor the blood that Adrian could see seeping from beneath the rail. The thick nail had pierced Stu's hand.

"Can't lift it…"

"Hold on, hold on," Adrian told him, keeping his voice low and level. With both hands he lifted the broken railing, sucking in his breath at the damage the nail and the weight had done to Stu's hand. Stu yelped and then swore, clutching his injured hand close to him. Adrian let the rail fall and reached for his friend.

"Let me see." He shook his head and let out a curse at the sight. "No wonder you yelled. It went right through."

"Feels like it," agreed Stu, face pale from the pain.

"Looks like it missed the bone – doesn't seem broken," Adrian said, turning his friend's hand slightly to get a better look at it. "Bleeding like a stuck pig, though. We'd better get you to the house, and I'll send Bill for the doctor."

Stu shook his head. "I don't need a doctor. Just wrap it up. It'll be fine."

"Stu, this could cause some serious damage – damage your hand might not recover from. I can't just let you shine it on – even if does teach you to wear gloves. Didn't I tell you?"

Stu grunted.

"It wouldn't have stopped that rail from falling."

"No, but it might have cushioned you some." He shook his head again and put an arm around Stu to support him as they began to move, starting the walk toward the house. "Look, if you don't want to see the doctor, that's fine. Ma can fix you up some. She certainly knows how to bandage a wound."

"I would think so, raising you," said Stu, with an echo of his usual sense of humor showing through the pain.

"If you thank her nicely, she might even let you stay for supper."

"Supper sounds good, if I can use my hand to eat it – oh, no, Ade."

"What?"

"Clarabelle." Stu cried. "In all of this I plumb forgot about my sister. She'll be waiting at the station. Will you hitch up the horse, and I can go in for her now? She's going to think I forgot all about her."

"Come on, come on," Adrian soothed his friend, refusing to let him sidetrack and turn back toward the barn. "You're in no shape to drive, no matter whether I hitch up the mare for you or not. Come on into the house, and I'll go and fetch her for you."

His foreman turned a wide-eyed face to him, still pale from hurting, but already with gratitude rushing over it.

"Oh, would you, Ade? I'd be indebted to you."

"Sure," Adrian said, as they reached the stairs and he helped Stu up and over the last few steps to the back door of the house. "After all, you're practically like a brother to me – which makes your sister my sister, doesn't it? Come on in the house and don't worry about it. Let Ma see your hand. Don't be a baby, now…"

Izetta Moss greeted them with a worried expression and an exclamation when she saw the state of the foreman's hand. Phoebe, who came to see what the fuss was about as soon as she heard her mother's cry, rushed immediately to the stove to put the kettle on for hot water as Izetta reached for her basket of bandages and miscellaneous items for healing and patching up the various trials that befell the workers on the ranch. When Adrian left his friend, Stu was sitting with his mouth clamped shut tight, refusing to cry out as Izetta cleaned the blood from the wound and clucked at the depth of it.

Adrian shook his head and smiled to himself as he headed for the barn. He knew his friend couldn't be in better hands. His mother and sister would see to that.

In the meantime, he had another little sister waiting for him.

And someday soon, he reminded himself, he would be setting out to collect someone from the train station – only this time, it would be his bride.

CHAPTER 4

The brief twilight of early spring had already started to deepen into a youthful nighttime when the train got up steam and headed out of the station once more, leaving Clarabelle Demont standing all by her lonesome in the middle of the platform at Fort Riggins, Montana.

For a moment, she continued to stand there. It seemed impossible – but the evidence was difficult to deny. She had been waiting for over an hour now. The rest of her fellow travelers had come and gone, met by friends and family, or wandered off on their own to find the saloon or the inn or some other popular destination. She alone was left at the station, uncollected – and unwanted.

The thought was impossible to dismiss. Her brother had encouraged her to come here to Fort Riggins, it was true –

but perhaps he hadn't really thought she would take him up on it. Perhaps it had been nothing but a polite invitation of the sort that seems necessary to make at the time, but which is not really in earnest. Had she complained too much about being alone? Had she made him feel guilty and prompted him to offer a home even though he preferred her to stay where she was?

Was she not wanted at all?

The thought made her miserable. The journey from Ohio had not been easy, but with each hour that had crawled by, she had told herself that at least she had family waiting for her. She had pictured the scene of her arrival, of stepping off the train to find he had been waiting for hours, desperate to ensure he was not late. She had seen, in her mind's eye, how warm and welcoming it would be to rush into his brotherly embrace and feel that she was, once again, home.

The gravity-fueled tumble from the heights of her dreams brought her to the depths of reality. Her brother was not waiting for her. No one was waiting for her at all.

She was truly alone in the world.

"Now, Clarabelle Demont," she whispered to herself fiercely, stepping forward and heading to a bench to sit down, "you're being overly dramatic. Of course, he hasn't forgotten about you. Something must have happened. He's your brother – he won't simply leave you to sort things out for yourself. Just sit yourself down and make up your mind to wait."

Determined to do just that despite her misgivings, she took her seat. From her point of view, with her back to the empty ticket seller's booth, the rails stretched away in front of her to the right and to the left. On the far side there was nothing but an emptiness, wide fields with mountains in the distance, turning blue in the twilight. It was beautiful, strange, foreign territory, not quite like anything she had ever seen, and for a long few moments, she was caught up in a reverie, transported to – well, to somewhere else. She couldn't quite put her finger on it, but it fed a poignant ache in her soul.

Then there was the soft sound of someone clearing their throat to gain her attention.

She stood up swiftly, her heart thudding in her ears, and looked toward the source of the sound. It proved to be a man, tall and slim, with narrow shoulders and a well-cut frame. He stepped forward, and in the last dim light of day, she saw that he was handsome. Startlingly handsome – a square chin, a mouth that spoke of a good sense of humor, wide hazel-green eyes with black lashes, and a thick thatch of dark brown hair revealed as he took off his hat politely. His eyes met hers and for what seemed like forever, they stood and simply gazed at each other.

Clara's reverie as she looked at the strange landscape seemed not to have ended; rather, it was as though it had morphed into something different and provided this handsome stranger, part and parcel of the land around her, as much a product of her lonesome daydreaming as the echo of her heartbeat in her ears.

Then he cleared his throat again, softly, at last speaking to her.

"I don't suppose you're Miss Clarabelle Demont."

Hearing her own name dropping like an unexpected gem from the lips of the stranger sent a cold shock through Clara's middle, and she had to take a few seconds to recover before she could make her answer.

"Yes, I am," she managed. "Are you – did Stuart send you for me?"

The handsome stranger gave her a kind, somewhat rueful smile.

"As a matter of fact, he did," he said. "Your brother got – caught up with some matters at the ranch. He was terribly afraid you would think he'd forgotten all about you, so he sent me in his place."

It was a relief to her heart to hear that Stuart hadn't, in fact, forgotten, and that he was even worried she would believe that he had. Shouldering past that sense of relief, however, was a stronger sense of curiosity about the man he had entrusted to collect her instead.

"Do you – work at the ranch with Stuart?"

Another smile, the man's teeth gleaming in the light.

"I do," he said. "Matter of fact, we work very closely together. Stu is an old friend of mine – I've known him since he started there." He held out a hand to her. "I'd be glad to take you to him, if you're ready to get out of this empty station. My – the lady of the house back at the ranch has some supper waiting for you, and a cup of tea, too."

The idea of supper and a cup of tea sounded overwhelmingly wonderful to Clara. The abrupt end to her fears of being forgotten and neglected, after so long of feeling alone, brought the faint beginnings of emotional tears to her eyes. The handsome stranger seemed to perceive them at once, and stepped forward, putting his hand on her arm.

"Here, now," he said, his voice soft and gentle. "What's the problem, Miss Clarabelle?"

"Oh, I just – I'm just tired, I suppose." She wiped the tears away and smiled muzzily up at him. He smiled back, and she felt a surge of warmth pour over her heart like the man standing beside her was the sun itself.

"Well, I know the best cure for that," he said. "Supper, tea, a hug from your favorite brother, and an early bedtime. Is this your trunk? No, don't worry, I can manage just fine." He hoisted the trunk easily onto his shoulder, belying the slimness of his frame, and held out his other arm to her. Timidly, she slid her arm through the crook of his elbow and followed along with him.

"Ranching must make a man terribly strong," she ventured. "It took two of the porters to get the trunk off the train for me."

"Maybe," he agreed, with a grin. "Or maybe bein' a porter makes a man terribly weak. I've never had the chance to be a porter, so I can't say one way or another."

"I don't mean to downplay them, of course – they were very helpful."

"I'm glad. It must have been rough, gettin' all the way here from Ohio and finding no one was waiting for you. I should hope someone would have been kind to you."

"Everyone was very kind." In fact, it had seemed that no one particularly noticed her, but she couldn't bring herself to say a word of complaint to this man. He loaded the trunk into the back of the waiting buggy and then handed her up into the driver's box. His hand was warm and firm, and his touch sent tingles all the way down to her toes.

Then he was sitting in the box beside her and clucking to the horse. They began to move through the darkening streets, and she looked up to the expanse of the Montana skies.

"Cold?" asked the handsome stranger, putting his arm back behind them and brushing her arm in the process. He brought up a lap rug and draped it over her. "It chills down mighty fast once the sun goes down."

"Thank you. Er – what matters did Stuart get caught up in? I suppose it must have been terribly important?"

He glanced over sideways at her and seemed to be mulling over his words, choosing them carefully.

"If he had been able to come for you, he would have," he said at last, obviously choosing the route of reassurance, for which she was grateful. Was her worry of being left alone still that clear on her face? She would give herself a furrow between her brows deep enough to plant corn in if she didn't stop frowning. With an effort, she attempted to smooth out her expression, and managed another smile at him.

"I'm sure."

"There was a little bit of a disaster, I guess you'd say. See, another fellow – I won't name names, for I'm sure you'll meet him – made a mistake on the fencing. And Stu had to clean up after him, so to speak."

"Ah. I see." She was quiet for a moment. "No one else could have done that?"

"Not as well as Stu. He's the foreman for the ranch, you know."

"Yes – he told me. He's good at it, I'm sure."

"Sure is."

"And what does his boss think of him? Adrian Moss, the owner of the ranch?"

The handsome stranger took another moment to pick through his words carefully.

"Well, I reckon Adrian Moss thinks the world of Stu, as a matter of fact. You have every reason to be proud of your brother, Miss Clarabelle."

She couldn't help but smile at that.

"Thank you," she said. "I had thought it must be something like that." Finally at ease regarding her brother, she looked about them at the darkened countryside, lit only by the moon and the stars. "It's such a beautiful evening."

"It is, that. I hope you enjoy living here in Fort Riggins, Miss Clarabelle."

"If everyone is as nice as you have been, I'm sure that I will."

This earned her another smile as he turned off the road onto a smaller track.

"Nearly there, now."

"Circle Moss," she read from the signpost. "Is that the name of the ranch?"

"It is. Named after the family, of course – a little bit of a joke, since the town is Fort Riggins. The Moss family has been here for two generations now, and Gerald Moss named it when he came here all those years ago and started the ranch up with just a handful of sorry-looking cows."

She chuckled at his description. Her heart felt lighter and happier than it had for months; but there was something odd about the way she was feeling, too. The dreamy sensation she had experienced earlier had never quite dissipated, and she had half a mind to ask him to pinch her to see if she was dreaming.

"There it is," said the handsome man at her side softly, and she looked ahead to see the well-lit sprawl of the Circle Moss ranch house, oil lamps lit in every window as though to welcome her home.

"It's beautiful," she said, involuntarily clasping his arm – and then drawing away hastily as she realized what she had done. But he didn't seem to mind, just giving her another gentle smile. "Thank you so much for collecting me and bringing me back, Mr. – oh, goodness, all this time and I didn't even realize that I never got your name?"

He laughed.

"That's quite all right," he said. "My fault for not introducing myself properly. I'm happy to be of service, Miss Clarabelle – and my name is Adrian Moss."

CHAPTER 5

All the while as he drove into Fort Riggins, drawing closer to the train station with every turn of the cart's wheels, Adrian pretended he was heading to collect Linda Emmerson instead of Clarabelle Demont.

It was a harmless fantasy and took nothing away from the joy Stu and Miss Demont would undoubtedly feel once she arrived. Could he be blamed for wanting to get on with his life and meet the woman he was going to marry? He looked forward to the prospect every day.

In the meantime, Miss Clarabelle Demont needed his assistance, and he was happy enough to oblige on Stu's behalf.

The sky was growing dark, and the town was quiet as he drove up to the steps of the station on the far side of town.

For a few moments, he almost thought that no one was there at all. Had she given up on waiting and left? Had someone offered to take her home?

But then he saw the slight figure seated on the bench with her back to the ticket booth.

She was little more than a shadow in the dim light, gazing in rapt reverie at the landscape spreading vast on the far side of the tracks. He stepped forward and coughed gently to catch her attention. In a fluid, graceful movement, she was standing, facing him now, and the light seemed to glow from her, illuminating her features.

She was a beautiful girl. Small, slim, delicate, with thick golden blonde hair piled high on top of her head, rogue tendrils escaping to fall to her shoulders and frame her heart-shaped face. She couldn't have looked less like Stuart Demont, and for a moment he doubted she could possibly be Clarabelle.

But when he asked, she answered in a voice that was simultaneously gentle and strong.

He had to admit to himself that the rest of the evening passed by in something of a blur. He knew he must have helped her with her trunk, and she was very grateful. She asked him questions about Stu; he answered as best as he knew how. When she asked about what had kept her brother from coming to collect her, he took a moment to think before he answered.

If he told her the truth right away, she would only worry. It was obvious from the look in her eyes when he had first arrived that Stu's concern over her was well founded: she had thought she might have been forgotten. He'd done his best to reassure her that it couldn't be further from the truth. But telling her Stu had suffered an accident and was being patched up by Adrian's mother back at the ranch wouldn't be the best course of action either – would it?

She seemed to accept his renewed reassurance that Stu would have come for her if he could, and it settled in Adrian's mind that he'd made the right decision. Every now and then, as they drove toward the ranch, he glanced sideways and caught her staring up at the skies. The poor thing must be exhausted, he thought warmly. She needed to get back to the house before she found out about Stu; then she could reassure herself immediately, with her own eyes, that he was perfectly all right.

Adrian caught himself glancing sideways at the pretty young woman more and more often as the journey wound to a close. He could scarcely wrap his mind around the fact that this young creature next to him, with the wide blue eyes and the appealingly open face, with the slim yet feminine figure and the soft, gentle voice, could possibly be the sister that Stu had spoken about. She was too pretty…

With a jolt, he realized the real impact of the words that were whirling through his mind. Yes, she was pretty – very pretty – but he was practically an engaged man. He had no right to be noticing such things. The thought of Linda Emmerson, and of the ever-approaching day of her arrival, flushed his face embarrassingly red. In the darkness, luckily, Miss Demont did not notice.

In the end, as they arrived, it was just as much of a surprise to Adrian as it evidently was to Miss Demont that they had not yet been formally introduced. Adrian felt as though he'd known her for years; it seemed impossible they should be so comfortable with a girl he'd only just met.

Well, he told himself as he handed her down from the buggy, that just went to show what it could be like for him. That was exactly what Mrs. Gibbons had promised, wasn't it? Practically love at first sight…

Not that he had fallen in love with Clarabelle Demont, he amended to himself hastily. No, that wasn't what he meant…

But the feeling that he had with her. Surely, he would have that with Linda Emmerson as well. He just had to be patient and wait.

In the meantime, Miss Clarabelle had slipped her arm through his again. Glancing down at her, he was surprised to perceive she appeared to be nervous.

He squeezed her arm close to his side and smiled at her.

"Everything is going to be just fine," he whispered.

She smiled up at him gratefully and walked alongside him to the front door of the ranch house.

The moment the door was open, it seemed the world became a flurry of activity. There was Izetta Moss, welcoming Clarabelle into their home. Phoebe bustled around in a businesslike way, fixing the last details of supper and asking excitedly how the trip had gone; his younger sister had always been taken by the romance and adventure of train travel, and had not yet had the chance to experience it for herself. From the kitchen, there came a call.

"Is that my little sister?"

Clarabelle's head went up, and her eyes took on a sparkle.

"Stuart?"

Though a newcomer to the house, she fairly flew down the corridor toward the source of the voice. Grinning, with one arm around his ma's shoulders and the other around Phoebe's, Adrian followed her in time to see her fling her arms around her brother and embrace him.

The reunion between the two was beautiful to see. Adrian was surprised to see Stu's eyes closed tightly, with a few tears rolling slowly toward his beaked nose.

"Well, now," Stu said eventually, putting a hand on his sister's shoulder and putting her back a step. He cleared his throat noisily. "Let me look at you."

She obeyed, but the distance between them was all it took for her to realize something was wrong.

"Stuart. What on earth happened to your hand?"

"It's nothin'," he said, trying to tuck his injured arm behind the back of the chair on which he sat. Adrian came forward as his mother reached for the final table settings, and took his foreman's arm in his grasp, eyeing the bandage that covered the entirety of the hand.

"Doesn't look like nothing, does it, Miss Clarabelle?"

She turned a slightly accusatory glance on him. "Is this the 'matter' that kept him at home? You should have told me, Mr. Moss."

Adrian raised his eyebrows at her. "I didn't want to worry you."

"Goodness," she said, but she said it in a way that suggested other words had come to mind, words she would not allow herself to speak as a well-bred young lady. She shook her head at her brother and clucked.

"It's fine," said Stu, first to her and then to Adrian, as though desperate to convince anyone who would listen.

"It isn't fine at all," said Izetta from the other side of the table. Adrian's ma was a small woman, and not at all given to harshness, but there was a sharpness and a strength in her voice that was the result of years of practice gainsaying her rather stubborn son, as well as the other employees of the ranch. "I told him point blank that Doc Carson should come out and look at it – or he can take tomorrow off and go in, if he'd rather."

"It's not that bad," Stu said again. Adrian ran his fingers lightly over the bandage and his foreman immediately contradicted his own words by letting out a yelp.

"Sounds bad," Adrian said.

"Well, if you're gonna insist on poking at it…"

"At least Ma did a good job with the bandage." He set Stu's arm down again to rest on the table, carefully. "I wish you'd go in and see Doc Carson, Stu. It won't take long."

"Better to just let it alone, and let it heal on its own," Stu said stubbornly. Adrian glanced up at his mother, who shook her head.

"He's your foreman," she said.

Adrian looked to Clarabelle, who met his gaze and shook her head slowly.

"It's been a long time since I've seen my brother," she said, "but if I remember anything about him, it's that he hates having anyone fuss on him, especially doctors. If my guess is correct, you won't be able to say anything to convince him to do something he doesn't want to."

Despite the pain that he was clearly still suffering, Stu smiled widely and patted his sister on the cheek.

"There you go," he said. "I knew you would remember the important part."

Amid the chuckles, the general chatter, and the clatter and business of getting supper, Adrian couldn't help but think that perhaps Clarabelle's presence would be a good influence on her older brother.

Even if that same presence did make Adrian's own life infinitely more complicated.

CHAPTER 6

"Clara? Are you home?"

The question brought a smile to Clara's lips. She set down the dish she was drying and headed for the front door, which she had propped open to let in the beautiful spring weather. Phoebe Moss, seventeen and the younger spitting image of her mother, was coming up the stairs to the cottage.

"Why, hello, there. Won't you come in?"

Phoebe gave her a smile that looked so much like her brother's, it made Clara's heart clench briefly.

"I'd rather you came with me, if you don't mind," she said. "Ma and I are just about to start putting the apple pies together, and I know you said you wanted to help."

"Oh, yes, I do. I never did pick up the knack for apple pies – my Aunt Mabel was more of a cherry pie baker, and any apple pies we made never seemed to turn out right. Just a moment, I'll be right with you."

She kept Aunt Mabel's apron around her waist, ignoring the hook just inside the kitchen, and cast a swift glance around her surroundings to make sure that everything was in place. Stuart was off working, of course, but if he should happen to come home before she returned from the ranch house, she hated to think that it would be messy.

Not that it hadn't been rather messy when she had first arrived…

It had been a week now since she had first set foot in her new home. A full and rather overwhelming week: Stuart was as loving as he knew how to be, but the age gap and the long time that had passed since they had last seen each other couldn't help but cause some awkwardness. She was immensely grateful for the support and friendliness of Phoebe and Izetta Moss. Adrian's sister and mother had reached out and made her feel welcome from the very moment she had arrived on Circle Moss Ranch.

And then there was Adrian himself, of course…

Hastily, she pushed the thought of him away for the moment and returned to the front door, where Phoebe waited patiently. If she thought too much of Adrian, she was bound to start blushing. And if she started blushing, Phoebe was bound to notice and ask her why. And she couldn't bring herself to tell Phoebe Moss that she had developed quite a wild crush on her older brother. She just couldn't.

She could hardly admit it to herself.

The fact was, however, despite her attempts to sidestep the issue, whenever there was a chance that Adrian Moss would be around, her heart rate went up and her mouth went suddenly dry. And as friendly as Phoebe and Izetta were, inviting her over to the ranch house every single day since she had arrived in Montana, there was always a chance that Adrian would be around. Sometimes, Clarabelle felt as though she were living in a constant state of ecstatic exhaustion.

Phoebe looped her arm through that of her new friend as she came down the steps and headed off in the direction of the ranch house, her eagerness causing Clara to have to skip to keep up with her taller friend.

"I just can't wait for the spring dance," she said. "Ma says at least half of the pies we're making will be allotted for the dance – of course, I can't help thinking that it's a little silly."

"Silly? Why?"

"Because no one goes to the dance to eat pie."

Clara laughed.

"I think you may be selling your ma's pies a little short," she said. "Everything that she makes is wonderful."

"That's all well and good, but we can eat pie whenever we want. The spring dance, on the other hand, only comes around once a year. Do you know, last year Ma told me I was too young to have a dance card – I had to stand around with the other children, and the band only played a few tunes that were just for us? I couldn't have a partner, I just had to dance with the rest." Phoebe shook her head. "You can bet I'm going to make up for it this year."

"I believe you," said Clara fervently. As sweet and unassuming as Phoebe appeared to be upon first acquaintance, there was no doubt that the young woman housed the soul of a firecracker deep within.

Phoebe led her up the stairs to the sprawling ranch house. Clara couldn't help a sigh of contentment as she stepped inside. As comfortable as her brother had tried to make the cottage, it was rather small and sparsely furnished; the absence of a feminine influence was patently obvious. The ranch house, on the other hand, was well-kept and well-appointed. It felt like – well, it felt like a family lived there. And it was based on the truth. Clara had never met anyone quite like the Moss family.

"Clarabelle. Please, come in, dear. The kettle is hot, pour yourself a cup of tea if you like. I'm just getting the dough from the cold room – it needs to be kept chilled if it's going to come out like it should."

Izetta Moss busied herself at the table, and Clara took a seat beside her, watching avidly as the older woman practiced her art. It was something to see – Aunt Mabel had been a good woman, that was undeniable, but a skilled cook she was not, even if Clara felt a bit guilty over admitting as much to herself.

An hour went by as Clara watched, then dug her hands in and helped. Izetta gave her pointers, and Phoebe offered teasing and occasional helpful criticism. As the day wound on, pie after pie appeared as though by magic, each taking a turn in the oven, crusts going from pale taupe to golden brown. A delicious smell permeated the kitchen, and Phoebe took a deep breath.

"Are you sure they're all for the dance, Ma?" she said hopefully. "Seems like we should try one – or two – just to make sure that they turned out all right."

Clara couldn't help but laugh.

"As though you don't eat enough of the pies that I make for us here at the house," Izetta said, shaking her head and chuckling. "It won't be long, now, dear, and you can eat to your heart's content – if we can tear you away from whoever you're dancing with at the time."

"Oh, I'm not going to be able to eat a bite at the dance. I'll be too excited. Won't you be excited, Clara?"

Clara smiled as she made another pass with the rolling pin. "I'm sure it will be just as exciting as you say, Phoebe – but I imagine I'll have plenty of time to have a bite or two of pie."

"No, you won't," said Phoebe. "You'll be dancing the night away, just like me."

"I don't know about that." Clara shrugged, keeping her eyes down. "Nobody knows me here – would any man really ask me to dance?"

"Of course, they will." The reply came from both Phoebe and Izetta at the same time, as both Moss women looked up at Clara indignantly. Clara raised her eyebrows at them, fighting a smile at their absolute certainty, which allowed no room for question.

"You're a beautiful girl, and you'll be with us," said Izetta, returning her attention to the oven.

"Besides," said Phoebe pragmatically, "I don't think you quite realize how few and far between the unmarried girls are here in Fort Riggins – in most of Montana, really. Why do you suppose Adrian hasn't gotten married before now? Or your brother, for that matter?"

The casual mention of Adrian as a bachelor was enough to bring another blush to Clara's cheeks, but she pushed past it and chose to focus on the other subject: that of her brother.

"Has he really never courted anyone?" she asked, automatically dropping her voice low as though he might be listening at the door. "Aunt Mabel always suspected that he was simply hiding his attachment from us until he was engaged – but then he never said anything about any girl in particular."

"Your brother is as confirmed a bachelor as I've ever met," Izetta stated firmly. "And I've known a few in my time."

"Oh, I don't know," said Phoebe. "Stu puts on a big show of being perfectly happy the way he is – but I can't imagine that he'll never allow any pretty girl to turn his head. That's what everyone wants, isn't it? To find someone, settle down, and be happy." She poked at the dough in front of her experimentally. "That's how we were made."

"I can't argue with that," Clara acknowledged, softly. For a moment, she allowed herself the indulgence of contemplating the possibility of Adrian walking into the room, right now, giving a fond embrace to his mother and sister and a smile, just as fond, to Clara herself. The thought traced warm fingers up her spine. She loved Adrian's smile – she couldn't deny it. Every time he looked at her with that smile she felt as though she were being wrapped in a warm blanket.

And she thought there was the possibility, however remote, that Adrian might feel somewhat the same about her in return.

Oh, she had nothing really solid upon which to base this thought – it was more hope than anything. But he had been very friendly and welcoming to her from the very beginning. Was it possible she could feel such a strong connection between them, and he felt nothing at all? Why, then, did he smile at her so often, and with such warmth?

After living on the premises of Circle Moss for only a week, she realized suddenly that she was in great danger of losing her heart to its owner.

With an effort, she pulled herself back to the reality that was right in front of her: Izetta at the oven, Phoebe chattering away, and a veritable mound of pie dough just waiting for her attention. With a faint sigh, she re-applied herself to the task at hand.

"But what do you think, Clara? Will you help me?"

Clara looked up at Phoebe, realizing guiltily that her own daydreams had kept her from hearing a word the younger girl had said.

"Of course, I'll help you," she said, belatedly. "Er – when shall we start?"

"Why, this afternoon would be best, if Ma will spare us from the kitchen," Phoebe said, darting a glance at her mother. "What do you say, Ma?"

Izetta eyed her daughter with a serious gaze.

"Now, Phoebe. The flowers are important for the dance, but do you really think it's necessary to head out and start picking 'em right this minute? They'll wilt and fade long before they're ever seen."

"We don't need to pick them all today," Phoebe cajoled her mother. "But we should at least head out and see what there is. We'll start with the south meadow, and maybe there will be enough there for some wreaths and daisy chains. But supposing we have to search further afield?"

"I reckon there'll be plenty in the south meadow. The way this spring has been going, greenery has sprung up all over."

"But just supposing, Ma, that we have to go over to town to look for flowers." There was a definite wheedling tone in Phoebe's voice now, and Clara smothered a smile. "Think of the time it'll save if we find out now."

There was a pause – the sort of pause that suggested that Izetta was drawing out her permission as long as it would go in order to keep her daughter on her toes.

"Well, all right, then," she said at last, and when Clara's eyes met hers, she gave her a discreet wink. "But mind you're back by supper, I don't relish having to come after you in the cold dark.'"

"It's hardly cold anymore at night," Phoebe countered, but she was too busy undoing her apron to really put any strength into her argument.

"Never mind your gainsaying. Just be back by suppertime."

"We will, Ma. I promise." Phoebe pecked her mother on the cheek and then slid her arm through Clara's, drawing her toward the kitchen door. As they went, the younger girl chattered on about the task ahead, mercifully filling in the gaps in Clara's attentiveness.

"I'll be honest, I couldn't quite believe it when they asked me to take charge of the flowers for the dance. After all, a year ago I wasn't even old enough to attend by myself, and here I am with all this responsibility. But of course, everyone knows that the best flowers in Fort Riggins grow wild in the meadows of Circle Moss. So I suppose it makes sense that they'd ask me – still, it's a big responsibility, isn't it? I'm so glad you're willing to help."

"Of course, I am," Clara said firmly, squeezing Phoebe's arm close to her side. "Just tell me what to do, and I'll do it."

"Well, here's what I was thinking…"

As they made the long walk toward the south meadows, where the prettiest flowers were bound to be found, Clara listened to Phoebe's outline of her plan for the decoration of the town hall. Inwardly, she took stock of her situation and marveled at it. Just a short week ago she had been feeling absolutely alone, with no one in the home beside her, no one to talk to, no one to pay her any attention – no one to whom she could show love. Now, here she was, living with her brother for the first time since she was a child. And it was more than just her blood-related family – it was the Moss family, too. Phoebe and Izetta had taken her under their wing as swiftly as though she were a long-lost daughter. And as for Adrian…

Well. She gave a faint sigh, hoping that Phoebe wouldn't notice. Luckily, her friend was too deeply involved in the details of how to connect the daisy chains with the sprays of purple shooting stars to pay her any heed.

As for Adrian, she could do little more than hope.

Only time would tell.

CHAPTER 7

The object of her single-minded attention was deeply engrossed in a similar task of his own – trying to keep his mind off Clarabelle Demont.

No matter how hard he tried, it seemed to stray back again and again. Every time he closed his eyes, the pale, luminous, beautiful face of the ranch's newest guest floated up out of the darkness before him.

And even as he tried to redirect himself, to focus on the task ahead, to think of the immediate future and the hopes he held so dear, the truth kept coming back to him.

No matter what Mrs. Gibbons had promised him, he could not rid himself of the feeling of regret over the fact that Linda Emmerson was even now on her way in his direction.

The very thought caused such a deep sigh that the calf he was tending to gave him a startled glance. He was out in the south field, re-introducing the mother and her baby to the herd. It was not usually a very involved process, but things were complicated by the initial poor health of the calf. The poor little thing had a bad leg and was not able to walk as freely as the rest in its age group, who had long since been released back with the others. Adrian and Stu had taken it in turns to watch over and work with the little fellow, and it had gradually grown strong enough to be finally allowed to start its life in the meadows.

With a fond smile twisting at his mouth, Adrian slapped the calf gently on the rump, sending it to gambol toward its mother, who was heading steadily in the direction of her long-lost sisters. Adrian stepped through the south gate and closed it behind him, then leaned his elbows on it to watch the animals for a while. He gave another deep sigh, but it was a bit more contented this time. There was nothing quite as peaceful and reassuring as the sight of his herd living their lives to the full on his beautiful ranch.

That was what he wanted – a life as peaceful and full of joy and contentment as was being enjoyed right in front of him. Was that too much to ask?

He couldn't help but fall back on pondering over what Mrs. Gibbons had told him. She had practically guaranteed him love at first sight. But suppose that he had already fallen in love?

The question was wayward, errant, and caught him by surprise. He shied away from it – but then approached it again, driven by an irrepressible curiosity. He couldn't be in love with Clarabelle Demont – could he? He'd only known her for a week. And yes, she was sweet and kind and beautiful. Yes, they got along better than he could have ever hoped for. And yes, she was unattached to any man, so far as he knew. He even loved Stu like they were already brothers.

Could he really hope to find anything better in the long-awaited person of Linda Emmerson?

It didn't matter in the end, and he knew it. He had hitched his wagon to the promise of Linda Emmerson. He owed her – he had given his word they would court with a view to being married. They were practically engaged as it was, and they hadn't even met yet.

When she arrived in a few short days, he had a feeling his fate would quickly be sealed.

Hazel eyes still fixed on the peaceful herd grazing in front of him, he shook his head.

"It's your own fault, Ade," he muttered.

He pushed himself away from the gate and took his horse by the reins. It was a long way back to the barn, but it was a beautiful afternoon, and the walk would do him good.

He was cresting the slight hill that interrupted the path to the south meadows when he first heard the sound of laughter. Adrian froze for a moment, puzzled – but then the sound came again, and he recognized the unmistakable sound of his sister's voice, raised in jollity and teasing.

He grinned to himself and headed on.

He reached the top of the hill well before they realized that he was there. Looking down over the draw in front of him, he saw his sister accompanied by Clara Demont.

It was undoubtedly her. That crown of golden hair. That slim, elegant figure. The way she threw her head back to laugh at something his sister said, full of life and vibrancy. Like nothing and no one he had ever known.

His heart twisted within him, and he fought off the surge of longing – swiftly followed by an even larger swell of guilt.

Gritting his teeth and clenching his jaw, he continued down the draw to meet them, calling out with enforced cheeriness.

"Hello, girls. What are you up to?"

Their laughter stopped, but only for a moment as they looked his way. Then there was another bout of giggles, and he clearly saw Phoebe elbowing Clarabelle in the ribs. The older girl controlled herself quickly, however, and greeted him with a friendly smile.

"Hello, Mr. Moss. You find us in pursuit of our responsibilities."

"Oh?" He raised an eyebrow.

"The organization committee has put me in charge of the flowers for the dance," Phoebe said. "We're going to pick some in the south field. That's all right, isn't it?"

"Fine by me. The cattle might have something to say about it; they've got a sweet tooth for wildflowers."

By now they were quite close to each other, and Clara stepped forward to smooth her hand over his horse's nose, softly.

"What a sweet girl," she said. "This is Gemella, isn't it?"

"She is," Adrian said, nodding. "Old Gem, I call her – she's the oldest mare on the ranch, but one of the most reliable. I bring her out with the calves when I need a mount, she's gentle as a lamb."

"She looks it," Clara said. Her eyes met his, and he swallowed hard, though his mouth was suddenly dry. "I'm glad she's still of use, even if she is old."

"Ade," said Phoebe suddenly, "did you know Clarabelle has never been on a horse before?"

Adrian turned an inquiring glance on Clara, who was blushing faintly.

"Yes, it's true, though it's embarrassing enough to say it," she said. "My aunt and I lived in town, and we could walk everywhere we needed to. We never had a horse, and I never got the chance to ride."

"Well, that won't do," Adrian found himself saying. "You're living on a ranch now, Miss Clarabelle, and not in any town. You must have riding lessons."

"Will you teach her, Ade?" Phoebe asked, eyes wide with innocence. "He taught me," she informed Clara, "and I'm positive that's why I've only ever fallen off a horse twice."

Adrian grinned at his little sister.

"That was your own fault," he said. "If you had just listened to me…"

"Oh, dear," murmured Clara, brows furrowing with concern. Adrian turned his gaze back to her and only just restrained himself from bursting into laughter.

"Don't you worry, Miss Clarabelle. You and my sister are pretty different – I reckon you know what 'hold on tight' means." He took a renewed hold on the reins. "Of course, I'll give you lessons, if you want 'em. Matter of fact…" He glanced swiftly up at the mare, and then back down at Clara. "Come on over here, and we'll start right now."

"Oh, but I couldn't take you away from your work."

"I've just finished my task for this afternoon. All I've got to do now is muck out the barn, and Lord knows I don't mind postponing that as long as I can. Come on over here, Miss Clarabelle."

Clara exchanged glances with Phoebe, who nodded encouragingly, and did as she was told.

"I don't know that I…that is, I wasn't exactly planning…"

"Hold on here – good – now just hold your breath and think lightly."

In the next moment, he had lifted her up in the air and deposited her solidly on Old Gem's back. With a slight squeak of surprise, she gripped the pommel of the saddle tightly, and he took her ankle in his hand, arranging her foot in the stirrup.

She looked down at him, and he froze, caught in her gaze like a mouse in a trap. His hand was still on her ankle, and he could feel the fine and delicate bone beneath his fingers, just above the top of her buttoned shoes. He saw her swallow, as though it was painful for her, and realized suddenly that holding fast to the ankle of a young woman was not the most gentlemanly thing to do. Hastily he let go, and without thinking about it, swung himself up in the saddle behind her.

"Goodness," said Clara, breathing heavily.

"We'll just take a little jaunt toward the south meadow," he said, reaching around her to take up the reins. She was so warm – it felt so right to have his arms around her – why on earth had he decided to apply for a Mail Order Bride when Clara was mere days away from entering his life? In his mind, he flung curses at himself for his impossible shortsightedness. Out loud, he murmured soothingly to both the mare and to Clarabelle. "Everything's going to be just fine."

"Hey there," said Phoebe, still down on the ground, putting her hands on her hips. "What about me?"

Adrian tossed her a grin.

"You already know how to ride," he said, and turned Old Gem with a skilled nudge at her ribs and a tug on the reins. It was the work of a few seconds to coax the old mare into a canter, and when Clara let out a small cry of distress, he held onto her all the tighter.

"See you at the south meadows." he called over his shoulder to his sister.

Then it was just the three of them – Old Gem, Clara, and Adrian himself – in the simultaneous noise and silence, peace and frenzy, of riding together through the beautiful day, following the path south with a surety that eluded them in every other aspect of their lives.

CHAPTER 8

Clara Demont thought about that horseback ride for days afterward.

She had a feeling she was going to continue to think about it for years.

It wasn't just the ride itself, though that was glorious enough. Once she had gotten over her initial fear and trepidation, she had forgotten about the jouncing and the jostling that came with riding horseback and focused instead on the feeling of the wind in her hair, the sun on her face, the gorgeous world rushing by. The mare had not gone too fast, and she had never feared control would be lost.

But more than that was the solid warmth at her back, the tightening of the arms around her – more than that was Adrian Moss.

She couldn't quite put her finger on what had prompted him to take her up in the saddle that day. She had a funny feeling he wasn't quite sure himself. It was the act of a man who was behaving strictly on impulse, rather than by plan. They had not spoken as they rode south to the flower meadows; there was no chance to do so, unless they wanted to shout out and try to top the sound of the wind and clatter-thud of horse hooves.

There was just the two of them – and the ride.

They had arrived at the meadow all too quickly for Clara's taste. Old Gem slowed to a trot, and then stopped altogether, and Adrian slid down from her back immediately. Clara missed his embrace at once, but he turned his face to look up at her and gave her a smile.

"What do you think?"

She shook her head at him.

"I'm afraid I feel – quite speechless."

"Ah, well. Phoebe will cure you of that, just give her a chance." He grinned at her, and one hand came up to cover hers on the pommel of the saddle. "Learning to ride is important here on the ranch – I hope you take to it as well as you've taken to everything else."

"Do you think I've taken well to things?"

"Ma says you're the best help she's ever had in the kitchen. Of course, her only point of reference is Phoebe, so maybe that's not sayin' much." His eyes were teasing. "Still, I know she's glad to have you around. So is Phoebe. So is your brother."

It was too much for her to bear.

"And you?" she asked, trying to keep the eagerness from her voice.

His eyes met hers. Slowly, he nodded.

"So'm I," he said. "Speaking of which – you might as well start to call me Adrian, Miss Clarabelle, instead of Mr. Moss. We're going to be friends, you and I."

"Yes," she said, gratefully. "And you – you can call me Clara, if you like."

"That's what Stu calls you, isn't it?"

"Yes. It was my family name."

She was not imagining the gratification in his smile.

"Then that's what I'll call you," he said, and helped her down off the horse.

The rest of the afternoon had flown by in something of a blur. Once Phoebe arrived – not long after, having run all the way, though she complained loudly of a stitch in her side – Adrian mounted the mare and headed back in the direction they had come, leaving the two young women to their task. Phoebe conducted a businesslike assessment of the range, variety, and plenitude of the south meadow wildflowers, and set Clara to picking a few bouquets "for demonstration purposes." Clara was glad enough to have something to do, something with which to occupy her hands, for her mind was in a positive whirl, and she could seem to see nothing but Adrian Moss everywhere she looked.

Not that she minded…

"We're going to be friends, you and I," he had said. Did he mean it? Did he mean just friends – or something else? Was it possible he felt much the same way about her as she felt about him?

Oh, there were too many possibilities and not enough certainties, and she had never felt so gloriously distracted in her entire life.

Now here it was, Saturday afternoon, and with Phoebe giving directions, the masses of flowers the two of them had collected were being put into place. Clara arranged a final bouquet in a glass jar and stood back to look at it critically. Her friend nudged her with her elbow and gave her a cheerful smile.

"Do you know what, Clara? I think we've done a terribly good job, myself."

Clara took a few more steps back and looked up at the town hall. It was the largest building in Fort Riggins, and handsomely appointed. The elegant lines were made more appealing by the generous application of flowers and greenery; everywhere she looked, it seemed there was a wreath, a daisy chain, or a bouquet in whatever donated glass container they could scrounge. It was absolutely beautiful, and the epitome of spring.

She smiled.

"I think we have, too." On impulse, she threw one arm around her young friend and gave her a hug. "Thank you for asking me to help."

Phoebe hugged her back.

"Thank you for being willing. Oh, Clara, I'm so glad you're here. Everything seems to be better with you around."

Her friend's unexpected words caught Clara by surprise, bringing tears to her eyes. After all the pain and loneliness of the last few months, the unquestioning acceptance by the Moss family couldn't help but reach her heart. It was so much more than she had expected – but so much like what she had been praying for.

"Goodness, look at the time." Phoebe snatched her by the hand. "Our dresses are waiting for us at Mrs. Meade's. Let's go, or we'll be late."

Held fast by the hand, Clara followed in Phoebe's wake, still smiling and trying to wipe away her tears.

CHAPTER 9

The annual spring dance was no disappointment on this particular year. Spring had started early, and the unseasonal warmth of the weather had led to a bumper crop of flowers and greenery. The town hall was bedecked with yellows, purples, and pinks, and the colorful dresses of the women only added to the dazzling array. All of Fort Riggins had turned out in their finest.

Adrian Moss, standing in the corner near to the table heavily laden with pies – most of them supplied by his mother – only had eyes for one beauty among the Sunday-best throng.

He didn't intend to be watching Clarabelle Demont, but it was almost as though he couldn't help himself. He could not tear his eyes away from her.

As diligently as every other person in the room had tried to dress up for this occasion, she outshone them all.

And he knew with a rather wretched feeling in the pit of his stomach, he was not the only man to have noticed. Far from it. Clarabelle Demont was surrounded by hopeful young men like hummingbirds surrounding an open-throated flower.

She certainly didn't seem to mind, either. Though he knew her to be a modest and down-to-earth girl, he didn't blame her for having her head turned a bit by all the attention. It was impossible to avoid, wasn't it? She'd never been in a situation quite like the spring dance in Fort Riggins, Montana.

Again and again, he turned his eyes away, seeking to focus on something, anything else – and again and again his eyes were drawn back to her, watching her dance with one man after another. At the very least, she didn't seem to favor any one above the other, but that was cold consolation.

More than once, he caught her tossing a glance his way. It made him hot and cold all at once, every single time, and he folded his arms and tried to keep his gaze from wandering toward her – it worked, but only for a short while.

What was he going to do about this? he asked himself plaintively. It was his own fault – he shouldn't have given her riding lessons a few days ago. Then he wouldn't have the memory of her in his arms quite so fresh in his mind...

But he had, and he did, and now he had to simply live with the consequences, as there seemed to be no solution.

All he wanted to do was to go to her, politely but firmly push aside whoever she was talking or dancing with at the moment, and hold out his hand for her to take…

But that was the one thing that he could not do. Not when Linda Emmerson was scant days away from arriving in Fort Riggins.

He was watching Clara again and stewing in his own confused misery, when his sister stepped up next to him. She had been making the most of her first outing at the spring dance, with nearly as many admirers to fill her dance card as Clara herself. Her cheeks were flushed, her hair coming loose, and her eyes sparkling. She nudged her older brother in the ribs.

"Go on, then," she said.

He turned a bland glance on her.

"Go on, what?"

"Go and ask Clara to dance. You've had the words between your teeth all evening, and if you don't spit them out you might choke on them."

Adrian stared at his sister. It was on the tip of his tongue to make some rude retort – but the truth was, he was painfully aware, that likely everyone had noticed him staring. He couldn't blame Phoebe for commenting on it.

Nor could he truthfully say he had no idea what she was referring to, which was his first inclination.

Instead, he squared his shoulders and lifted his chin. "I can't do that."

"Can't or won't?"

"Either one. Both. And you know it, Miss Phoebe."

She blinked at him, eyes wide with pretended innocence. "What do you mean?"

Adrian gritted his teeth.

"Come on, now. You're my sister. You're not supposed to make this harder on me than it is already."

"Aha, so you admit it. You fancy Clara, don't you?" Phoebe nodded enthusiastically, clearly pleased with herself. Adrian reached up and swiftly tugged at one of the locks of hair that had fallen loose.

"Why don't you just advertise it to the whole town? Goodness, for a girl who is as meek as milk around strangers usually, this dance certainly brings out a different side of you."

"It isn't as though they can't all tell anyway," Phoebe said, reaching up to tug at his much shorter hair in return, smartly. "Anyhow, I don't see what the problem is. You like Clara – why not go and ask her to dance?"

"Because, as I shouldn't have to remind you, I have a Mail Order Bride on her way even as we speak," Adrian said, turning away from her to face the crowd again and dropping his voice even lower. "She'll be here tomorrow afternoon, Lord willing and the creek don't rise. Regardless of how I feel about Clara Demont, it wouldn't be right to allow myself to – or to make her think – or to – it wouldn't be right."

Phoebe was staring up at him, and the wideness of her eyes was not a pretense, this time.

"Goodness, Ade," she said, finally dropping her voice low as well. "You really do like her, don't you?"

Adrian glanced toward his sister swiftly, and just as swiftly away. His heart churned within him, and the words he wanted to say simply would not come. Out on the dance floor, Clara laughed at something her partner had said.

"I'm in need of some fresh air," he said. "Tell Ma I'm headed home, will you? I'll walk, and Stuart can drive you home."

"Stuart's still in no position to drive, Ade…"

"Then you can manage, I'm sure."

"Adrian, you did tell Clara about Linda Emmerson – didn't you?"

He could not bring himself to answer. There was nothing he could do, nothing he could say, that would solve the dilemma in front of him.

"Go back to the party, Phoebe," he said. "Make the most of it while you're young."

He left her behind, staring after him with disappointment and sadness in her eyes.

CHAPTER 10

As the sun moved toward the horizon, the horse and cart clattered out of the drive, heading down the road that led to and from Circle Moss. Clara looked out the kitchen window, shielding her eyes from the sun.

"Phoebe, where is your brother going with the cart? I would have thought he'd have gotten anything he needed yesterday when we were all in town."

Phoebe was quiet for a moment, and Clara glanced over her shoulder in consternation. Now that she and the younger girl had become such close friends, she knew it was highly unusual for Phoebe not to reply to something right away.

"Phoebe? What is it?"

Phoebe was staring studiously at the bread dough as she kneaded it rather more enthusiastically than was warranted. She shook her head.

"I wish he would have told you this," she muttered. "But as he didn't – well, he's going into town, Clara, to collect someone at the station."

The way she said this otherwise innocuous sentence gave Clara a strange feeling in the pit of her stomach. She left the window and came to sit back down at the kitchen table, folding her hands in front of her and doing her best to be composed for whatever might come next.

"Someone?" she said. "A relative? A friend?"

"Neither, yet," said Phoebe, giving the dough a punch.

"I'm afraid I don't understand…"

"Her name is Linda Emmerson. We've never met her, but she's going to – well, she's going to stay with us for a while because…" Phoebe dropped all pretense of focusing on the bread dough and looked up at Clara beseechingly. "Because some time ago, well before you arrived, Adrian went to the matrimonial agency over in Hamilton, and they arranged for him to be matched with a nurse in Boston, Massachusetts. They've corresponded over the last several months, and now she's arriving on the train this afternoon."

An icy-cold hand gripped Clara by the heart. In a faint, far-off voice, she heard herself say, "A matrimonial agency?"

"Yes," Phoebe said, her face twisting a little in discomfort. "Oh, I wish he would have told you about it. I love my brother, but if he isn't the biggest chicken this side of the Mississippi, I don't know who is."

"He's – he's going to be married?"

"He's not engaged," Phoebe said hurriedly. "Not officially."

"But if he was matched by a matrimonial agency…"

"Yes – it's the next step, after Linda Emmerson arrives. If all goes well…I'm sorry, Clara."

Clara shook her head and looked down at the table. That explained it – that explained everything. It explained why, although he seemed to genuinely like her, he had not spoken of anything further in the few weeks they had gotten to know each other. It explained why at the dance last night he had not ventured over to ask her to allow him to partner her onto the floor. It explained so much – and yet it opened up even more questions as it laid some to rest.

Why had he been so very friendly with her? Why had he let her believe there might be something more?

And the answer, she told herself sternly, was he had done nothing of the sort. He had been nothing but polite. If she had read anything else into their relationship, it was her own fault.

If only she hadn't been so keen to feel loved. Perhaps she would have guarded her heart a little more from the very beginning.

Even so, while she could not allow herself to blame him, she had to acknowledge that if he had spoken up about his near-betrothal from the beginning, she would not even now be fighting off tears simply from hearing the news. The trouble was her initial crush on Adrian Moss had grown into something infinitely more. She loved the man deeply, all the more so as he suddenly seemed to recede out of her grasp.

"I'm sorry," said Phoebe, getting up from her chair and rushing around to throw her arms about Clara impulsively. "He should have told you. I should have told you. I know you were attached to him…"

Clara shook her head again.

"It doesn't matter," she managed, and put her hand on Phoebe's arm, grateful for the younger girl's unabashed affection. "It'll be all right – it's my own fault for thinking it might be something more."

"No, not at all. Adrian – my brother – I just wish he would talk to you, that's all."

"It doesn't matter now," Clara said again. She patted Phoebe's arm and stood up. "After all, if Miss Emmerson is arriving today, it's a useless point, isn't it?" Phoebe looked very much as though she had something she wanted to say but could not quite bring herself to speak the words; Clara smiled at her gently, sadly. "I'd better go out and see how my own brother is doing. He hasn't looked very well today."

"Yes – his hand was bothering him at the dance last night," Phoebe said, obviously grateful for the change in subject. "He couldn't even dance with me properly."

"I'll just go and make sure he's all right."

She managed to escape the kitchen before the tears began to flow.

For some time, she stood just outside the barn, back to the building, eyes to the sky, trying to will herself into a better grasp on her emotions. But her emotions were tricky things and evaded her each time that she thought she had them under control.

At long last, moved by the fear that at any moment she would hear the telltale sounds of the horse and cart returning, she turned and went into the barn.

"Stuart? Where are you?"

For a moment, she thought that perhaps he had already finished his work and headed to the next task. But then she heard his voice, faintly, coming from the back of the barn.

"Stuart? What are you doing? Are you all right?"

Her distress over Adrian giving way to concern for her brother, she followed the sound until she spotted him in the corner of the last stall on the left, slumped against the wall with his head leaning back. He gave her a weak smile and a wave as she came around the partition.

"'lo, Clarabelle…"

"Stuart, what's wrong?" She got down on her knees beside him and felt his forehead. "Oh, my goodness. You're burning up. Stuart, you've got a terrible fever – are you sick?"

He shook his head. His face was pale and sweat ran down his cheeks.

"Nope – 'm fine, just got a li'l tired and needed – needed a rest…"

The pitchfork he had been using to muck out the stalls lay discarded on the ground nearby. She looked her brother over in consternation, her eyes fixing on the bandage that was still wrapped around his hand. It had been a week and a half since he had injured himself while fixing the railing, and she had yet to see him remove the bandage entirely. Carefully, she took up his hand in one of hers and used the other to pull back the edge of the tightly-tied cloth. Stuart sucked in a breath in a hiss of pain, and she winced at the color of the skin beneath.

"Stuart, your hand looks to be terribly infected. That must be why you have a fever. We've got to get you into the house – can you stand?"

"'Course I can stand, silly," he muttered, and bent his knees as though to demonstrate. But his first attempt ended in him sitting back down with a grunt, and his second attempt did not even get that far. She tried to help him, draping his arm across her shoulders and lifting, but without his help he was nothing more than dead weight and her attempts had little, if any, effect.

"Stuart, I've got to go for help. Stay right here –"

He raised an eyebrow.

"—which you will, of course. Don't worry, everything's going to be just fine. I'll be right back."

She put a hand on his head, trying to comfort him, but her brother didn't appear overly worried; this was, no doubt, a sign of just how sick he really was, she realized as she hurried toward the entrance to the barn. In the distance, the cart was just pulling up to the front of the house.

Half forgetting Adrian's purpose in going to town, Clara rushed forward, calling his name at the top of her voice. In the distance, the trim figure that was Adrian Moss paused in the act of helping his companion out of the driver's box, his head turning toward her immediately.

"Clara? What is it?"

She raced up to them as quickly as she could, panting and breathless.

"It's Stuart – the wound on his hand is infected – he's very sick…"

Adrian put his hands on her arms, pressing firmly but gently, both a comforting touch and an encouragement to focus.

"Where is he, Clara?"

"In the barn – last stall…"

He was off, running so fast that his heels kicked up, leaving Clara behind to face the unknown woman who stood by the side of the cart. She was tall, much taller than Clara herself. Her hair was a dark auburn, pulled back so severely that the color was almost indeterminate under the stylish hat she wore. She was pretty, too – well, Clara thought hazily, that was as it should be. A man like Adrian shouldn't have anything less than a pretty wife.

The stranger held her hand out. "Linda Emmerson."

Biting her lip, Clara took it. "Clarabelle Demont. I'm – I'm very sorry."

Linda Emmerson shook her head.

"Don't be," she said. Her tone was clipped, but it seemed to be more for the sake of efficiency than any actual irritation. "Who is the wounded man?"

"My brother, Stuart Demont. He hurt his hand some time ago, and I'm afraid that he hasn't taken care of it as he should."

"Hmm," said Linda Emmerson, as though this was only to be expected. "He must be a bachelor. Any woman worth their salt would make sure the wound had been adequately cleaned."

Clara couldn't help but feel that this was a reflection on her, though she was his sister and not his wife. She hadn't paid much attention to it, really – was she partly to blame for his condition? If only she hadn't allowed herself to be so distracted by Adrian.

"He is a bachelor, actually," she managed. "A confirmed bachelor."

"Well," said Linda Emmerson, as though this in itself was doubtful. "I will say that I was myself a fairly confirmed bachelorette – until just recently. Times change our minds for us, don't you find, Miss Demont?" She turned to look at the barn and Clara followed her gaze. The two men were emerging, Stuart with his arm draped across Adrian's strong shoulders, leaning most of his weight on the younger man.

"Let Phoebe know," Adrian called to Clara as he came closer. "We'll put him in the spare room."

Clara nodded and dashed off to do as she was told. Phoebe was in the sitting room, frowning over a piece of mending that was giving her troubles. She was quick to abandon the piece and rush to set the spare room to rights – though, Clara suspected, there was nothing to set to rights, not really. After all, up until just a few moments ago, Linda Emmerson was intended to take up residence there. What would they do with her now?

When she came back to the front of the house, Adrian was carrying Stuart through the door and down the hall. For all Adrian's slim build, compared to Stuart's bulk, he seemed to have little trouble maneuvering the other man to the spare room. Stuart was put to bed, Phoebe pulling his shoes off for him, and covered up. His eyes closed before his head even hit the pillow.

"He's very sick," observed Linda Emmerson from just outside the doorway. She turned to Adrian. "He'll need care at once."

Adrian did not look at her. His eyes were fixed on Clara.

"I'll go for the doctor," he said. "It'll take half an hour, at least."

"I'm a trained nurse," Linda reminded them, stripping off her gloves and moving forward in a businesslike manner. "I will get his care started."

She shooed Adrian away from the bed, and he stepped closer to Clara. After a moment of hesitation, he reached out and put a hand on her shoulder.

"Don't worry," he said, softly. "Everything's going to be just fine. He'll be taken care of."

His reassuring words were enough to get straight past the defenses that Clara had only recently begun to build; she blinked back tears. Not trusting herself to speak, she nodded. In a moment, he was gone, and she was left there with Phoebe heading out to find her mother, Stuart turning restlessly in the bed, and Linda Emmerson, subjecting her to a long, thoughtful stare.

Clara met her gaze and lifted her chin. What was it about this unknown woman that made her feel so defensive? She was doing nothing but trying to care for her brother, after all.

"Let me know what to do to help," she said. "Anything."

Linda Emmerson paused a moment longer, and then nodded.

"Very well," she said. "Perhaps you can tell me what happened to your brother to lead him to this state."

"I wasn't here when it happened, but I've heard the details."

"That will be adequate, provided you are direct."

On the bed, Stuart shifted and turned his head. His black hair splayed out on the pillow, he opened black eyes and looked at the nurse. A smile creased his lips.

"Got m'self an angel," he murmured.

The words struck Clara oddly – she was torn between the urge to laugh and feeling appalled. But Linda Emmerson, strangely enough, seemed neither irritated nor offended.

Instead, she laid a surprisingly gentle hand on his forehead, leaning over him.

"That's right, Mr. Demont," she said soothingly. "Now go back to sleep."

He closed his eyes again, and she turned her attention back to Clara.

"Now," she said. "Tell me everything."

Clara took a deep breath and launched into the story, so far as she knew it.

Halfway through, she realized suddenly that she was scarcely paying attention to her own words; instead, she was listening keenly for the far-off sound of horse's hooves.

CHAPTER 11

In the days that followed, Clara Demont found herself wondering just what she had gotten herself into when she set foot on the train and started the journey that led her to Fort Riggins, Montana.

She couldn't regret it, despite everything. Here she was, hopelessly in love with a man who would any day now be announcing his engagement to another woman. Her brother had just been brought back from the brink of death. She had no other living family. She lived in a rented cottage that contained none of her own furnishings.

And yet, she knew there was nothing she would change. Hard times and tragedies had led her here – but if she had to go through them, this was where she wanted to be as a result.

Here at Circle Moss, here with Phoebe and Izetta and Stuart – and Adrian.

The subject of Adrian had continued to be a tricky one, but she was somehow thinking about it less and less. It wasn't any less painful now than it had been a few days ago when she first discovered he was practically engaged – but it occupied her thoughts much less frequently. She couldn't quite put her finger on why, except for the fact that Adrian himself was carrying on just as they had been before Linda Emmerson's arrival. Nothing seemed to have changed. He didn't seem to have any particular attachment to Linda. In fact, she'd scarcely seen them together since he had collected her at the train station.

And now, as the sun began to set, she found herself seated on the back porch of the ranch house, lost in thought. Thoughts about Adrian – about Stuart – about her future. What might happen – and what might not.

The sound of the screen door closing brought her out of her reverie, and she looked up to see Adrian himself smiling down at her.

"Penny for your thoughts?" he said. His hands were shoved deep in his pockets, and he looked relaxed, casual, as though they were old friends. The thought made her heart swell with gratitude. Somehow, despite it all, she had found the love she was looking for – and the good Lord had granted her far more than she had ever expected.

"I was thinking about my Aunt Mabel," she said, returning her gaze to the land spread out in front of her.

"Oh?" He took a seat beside her, stretching his long legs out on the porch.

"Yes. It's been three months now since she passed away."

"I'm sorry, Clara."

"So'm I – I miss her – but that wasn't what I was thinking about. I was thinking about how she poured herself into loving Stuart and me, even though we weren't her children." She paused for a moment, trying to organize her thoughts. "She never did have any children of her own – never got married. But when she had an unexpected chance to have a family, she didn't let anything get in the way of that. She raised us as best as she could and gave us all the love she had in her heart."

"I'm glad of that," Adrian said. "Every child should be raised with love. Even if it's not by their own parents."

"Yes, that's it exactly," she agreed, nodding.

"And what made you think of her?"

"I suppose I was thinking of how she set such a good example for me – and for Stuart, of course. A good example in loving whoever you have to love." She smiled. "Even if neither of us ever get married, that doesn't mean we won't have a family."

Adrian's hazel green eyes met hers frankly. "Don't you think you'll ever be married?"

"I wonder, sometimes."

"After the way all the men chased you around at the dance the other day? False modesty doesn't become you, Clarabelle Demont."

She laughed, but she was blushing at the same time. "I didn't even think about it like that. I enjoyed dancing with them, I admit. But as far as being courted…"

"Yes?"

She took a deep breath and forced herself to look away from him. Her hands were trembling, her heart was quaking. The truth was right there, ready to be spoken, but she could not bring herself to say it out loud.

"I suppose I'm a confirmed bachelorette," she managed at last, softly.

He was quiet for a long moment.

Then he said, "Never say never."

"I suppose it takes one to know one. After all, you and Nurse Emmerson…"

"Nurse Emmerson is right," he said, with a gentlemanly snort of amusement. "I've scarcely seen her since she arrived. She's been spending all her time with Stu – sometimes I think…"

The door was opened abruptly, cutting off his speculations. Clara looked over to see Phoebe standing there. Almost as though they had been caught in the act of something, a blush swept over Clara's cheeks.

But Phoebe didn't seem to notice. She had a funny look on her face, one that Clara could not quite place.

"Clara," she said. "Will you come to the spare room? Stu is asking for you."

"Oh, dear..." Clara stood up hastily and Phoebe put a hand on her arm.

"No, don't worry – he's perfectly fine. In fact, I'd say he's more than fine."

"What's that mean?" Adrian asked.

"Nothing," said Phoebe. "He's just – recovering quickly, that's all. Bouncing right back." She tugged on Clara's arm, and the older girl followed her into the house, mystified. As she stepped through the doorway, she threw a glance back at Adrian and met his puzzled gaze.

The question was answered, and immediately replaced by ten more when she opened the door to the spare room and stopped in shock at the sight that met her.

Her brother Stuart sat up, back propped against the headboard of the bed. Beside him, Linda Emmerson sat on the bed, demurely and calmly as though this were only natural. Between them lay their hands – clasped tightly.

Phoebe nudged Clara from behind, pushing her further into the room.

"Go on," she stage-whispered. "I want to hear all about it later."

Feeling rather numb, Clara stepped forward into the room.

"What on earth…"

"Clarabelle," her brother said, smiling as though all was right with the world, "I've got some news for you. Well. We've got some news for you."

"I – see."

"Yes," said Linda Emmerson, placidly. "It may seem highly irregular, but as a matter of fact you might be surprised at how often this sort of thing happens."

"What…sort of thing, exactly?" Clara wasn't entirely sure she wanted to find out, but the question had to be asked.

"I've asked Linda to marry me," Stuart informed her. His calm manner slipped for just a moment, and his grin turned wide and exhilarated. "And she said yes."

"I did," agreed Linda, as though her word was necessary to back up the truth of this statement. "I realize this is quite a short courtship to end in engagement this swiftly, but I'm sure you'll agree that as we're both a bit older, there's no point in waiting around once we've made up our minds."

"But…"

"Love at first sight," said Stuart rapturously. "Maybe you'll say it was the fever, but I know differently." His good hand squeezed Linda's tightly. "After all my protests about being a bachelor for good and forever, it turned out I just hadn't met the right woman yet after all."

Linda turned to look at him. The smile she gave him touched Clara to the heart – it was real, genuine, soft, feminine, and sweet. All traits she had not ascribed to the nurse up until now. But there they were, displayed for all to see, and brought on by her attachment to Stuart Demont.

But…

"But what about Adrian?" she managed at last.

"Yes," said Adrian from behind her. "What about him?"

She had been so distracted, and he had crept up behind her so softly, that she hadn't even realized he was there. She spun to meet him quickly – too quickly and took a step back. She nearly tripped in her haste, but he reached out a hand and caught her around the waist, bringing her to stand beside him. She looked up at him and he looked down, giving her a smile and a wink. It was obvious he was just as befuddled as she was, but the smile gave her courage, and the wink gave her a squiggly feeling in the pit of her stomach. Whatever was going on, they would find out together.

"About that," said Nurse Emmerson, standing up and stepping toward them. "I'm afraid I must end our courtship, Mr. Moss – but since we were never engaged, I don't feel it will be too much of a let-down for you. Besides which, I imagine you're perfectly happy to have the field open to pursue Miss Demont."

Adrian's eyebrows raised sharply. Behind Linda, Stu chuckled.

"Now, come on, Adrian. Everyone and their brother could see you were sweet on my little sister." Another chuckle. "Literally everyone and *her* brother."

"I don't…"

"Yes, indeed," said Linda Emmerson, calmly. "I could tell from the very first moment I arrived that your affections lay elsewhere. You scarcely spoke to me, we had no real connection, and each time Miss Demont was around, your eyes followed her everywhere she went. I harbor no ill will toward you at all for this, Miss Demont," she assured Clara. "I know it isn't your fault. In fact, I'm grateful to you both. You tried to do the right thing and hold to an agreement you'd made, even though it turned out not to be what you want. Well, I'm all for honorable actions, but in the face of the facts, it would be foolish in the extreme to pretend that our engagement was desired by anyone involved – and once

I set eyes on Stu, here," and she turned back to look at the patient fondly, "I saw clearly that the path forward must end our engagement – that is, yours and mine, Mr. Moss – and begin *our* engagement – that is, Stu's and mine. I do hope it hasn't been too confusing for all of you. I hate to be anything less than concise."

"I guess I…"

"Aw, come on, boss," said Stu. "You're not going to pretend you don't want to court Clara, are you? After all the work Linda put into explaining things?"

"Well, I…"

Adrian's mouth opened and closed a few times, but no further words came out. He reached up to scratch the back of his head and met Clara's gaze. She had been staring steadily at him throughout the previous exchange, quite unable to believe what was happening – and not at all sure that it *was* happening.

"Adrian?" she said softly since he didn't seem to be able to formulate any further sentences. "Perhaps we could speak in private for a moment?"

He nodded gratefully, took her by the hand, and they fairly flew out into the hallway.

Out from under the curious gaze of Stuart and Linda Emmerson, a bit of the energy seemed to flow back into him. Still, the words seemed to elude him. He planted her with her back to the wall, turned away and took a few steps, turned and paced back, looked at her, looked away, and then folded his arms and frowned.

Biting her lip to keep from smiling, she kept quiet and let him sort it out. She couldn't blame him for his discombobulation – it was terribly sudden. His officially unofficial engagement had suddenly been broken off by his Mail Order Bride, who was now marrying his foreman instead after only knowing him for a few days, part of which time he had been in a fever sleep. The only thing that topped this situation for sheer confusion was the fact that they had also apparently conspired to orchestrate Adrian's subsequent match to Clara. And all that in the span of a few days. While Stu had been sick in bed.

The laugh escaped her at last, and Adrian whirled around to face her once more.

"What's so funny?"

"Everything." she gasped. "Oh, my goodness, Adrian – what a story to tell our children."

It was a faux pas, a slip of the tongue, and something she had not intended to say. But the way his face lit up was something she would never forget.

He took her by the hand. "*Our* children?"

She couldn't go back on it, not now.

She smiled up at him.

"Yes. Our children. Our family," she said softly.

Adrian's eyes were lit from within.

"Do you know how much I love you, Clarabelle Demont?"

She threaded her arms about his neck.

"I'd love to hear all about it," she whispered, and then his lips met hers.

The End

CONTINUE READING...

Thank you for reading **Swapping His Bride!** Are you wondering **what to read next?** Why not read *Escaping the Marriage Contract?* **Here's a peek for you:**

Serena set the platter of hot, sliced roast beef on the table. The palpable tension emanating from her parents set her stomach to quivering. Her father's expression, as he never could hide his emotions, appeared a mix of anger, anxiety, and sorrow. Her mother wouldn't look her in the eye, her face downcast.

Serena slid her skirts under her and sat in her chair. The silence replacing the usual dinner table conversation unnerved her. *Has someone died? Surely Aunt Mae is in good health, for we visited her just last week.* Serena passed the bowl of mashed potatoes to her mother, Violet, hoping to see a lightening of her dour countenance.

"Is everything all right?" Serena finally asked. "You both seem – upset."

Violet flashed a glance at Michael, who grimaced. "Your father has something to tell you."

"All right." The quivering in Serena's stomach intensified. "It's not Aunt Mae, is it?"

"No," Michael answered, not meeting her gaze. "I'm not sure how to say this, Serena."

"Just say it," Violet snapped, her tone suddenly harsh, her brow furrowed in anger. "You got us into this wretched situation. It's your fault."

Serena gaped, pausing in the act of filling her plate with roast beef. She'd never heard her mother speak this way before. "What are you talking about?"

"I, er, made a bad business decision several years ago." Michael still wouldn't look at either of them, his elbows on the table as he clasped his hands together. "I went into debt. Deep debt."

"And?" Serena asked, tense, growing scared.

"The person I owed the debt to, in California, promised to cancel the debt if I, well, I –"

"Sent his only daughter and child to marry his son." Violet fairly trembled from bitter anger. "Your father agreed just today."

At first, Serena nearly laughed in relief. Surely this was a joke, a prank her parents were playing on her. An instant later, reality set in. Violet's anger was all too apparent, Michael's expression all too guilty.

"You can't mean it," Serena gasped. "I'm to pay your debt with my *life*?"

"It's not as bad as all that," Michael retorted, forking meat onto his plate. "You're twenty-one years old. It's high time you wed."

"But to a stranger? In *California*? A *stranger*?"

Visit HERE To Read More!

https://ticahousepublishing.com/mail-order-brides.html

THANKS FOR READING!

If you **love Mail Order Bride Romance, Visit Here**

https://wesrom.subscribemenow.com/

to find out about all **New Susannah Calloway Romance Releases! We will let you know as soon as they become available!**

If you enjoyed *Swapping His Bride*, would you kindly take a couple minutes to leave a positive review on Amazon? It only takes a moment, and positive reviews truly make a difference. Thank you so much! I appreciate it!

Turn the page to discover more Mail Order Bride Romances just for you!

MORE MAIL ORDER BRIDE ROMANCES FOR YOU!

We love clean, sweet, adventurous Mail Order Bride Romances and have a lovely library of Susannah Calloway titles just for you!

Box Sets — A Wonderful Bargain for You!

https://ticahousepublishing.com/bargains-mob-box-sets.html

Or enjoy Susannah's single titles. You're sure to find many favorites! (Remember all of them can be downloaded FREE with Kindle Unlimited!)

Sweet Mail Order Bride Romances!

https://ticahousepublishing.com/mail-order-brides.html

ABOUT THE AUTHOR

Susannah has always been intrigued with the Western movement - prairie days, mail-order brides, the gold rush, frontier life! As a writer, she's excited to combine her love of story with her love of all that is Western. Presently, Susannah lives in Wyoming with her hubby and their three amazing children.

www.ticahousepublishing.com
contact@ticahousepublishing.com

Made in the USA
Monee, IL
15 June 2022